Cheep Shot Murder

A Pet Shop Cozy Mystery

Book Eleven

By

Susie Gayle

Author's Note: On the next page, you'll find out how to access all of my books easily, as well as locate books by best-selling author, Summer Prescott. I'd love to hear your thoughts on my books, the storylines, and anything else that you'd like to comment on – reader feedback is very important to me. Please see the following page for my publisher's contact information. If you'd like to be on her list of "folks to contact" with updates, release and sales notifications, etc…just shoot her an email and let her know. Thanks for reading!

Also…

…if you're looking for more great reads, from me and Summer, check out the Summer Prescott Publishing Book Catalog:

http://summerprescottbooks.com/book-catalog/ for some truly delicious stories.

To sign up for our fun and exciting newsletter, which will give you opportunities to win prizes and swag, enter contests, and be the first to know about New Releases, click here:

https://forms.aweber.com/form/02/1682036602.htm

TABLE OF CONTENTS

CHEEP SHOT
MURDER

A Pet Shop Cozy Mystery Book Eleven

CHAPTER 1

"Here you go, and thanks for shopping at the Pet Shop Stop." I hand the young woman her bag and force a polite smile until she leaves. Owning and operating your own business is no small feat; owning and operating your own business while there's a murderer on the loose and you're ninety-nine percent sure you know who it is but you have no proof so the authorities won't believe you… well, that's a whole other ball game.

Still, we're trying. And by "we" I mean myself, my girlfriend Sarah, and her younger brother Dennis, the latter of whom has been uncharacteristically quiet these past couple of days—and reasonably so. Add to the mix that Sarah and I are in the process of closing on a house, and that she still has to tend to her duties as a Seaview Rock councilwoman, and you can see how life can get a bit hectic sometimes.

Oh, right. I should probably circle back around to that whole "murderer on the loose" thing. Long story short, a tree farmer here in town wanted to sell his land to a huge megastore corporation,

Sprawl-Mart, and then the very next day said farmer was found quite dead at our local watering hole. Despite a harsh warning from our police chief, I decided to investigate. (What's the use of being an officially licensed private investigator in the state of Maine if I can't, you know, investigate?) And what I discovered was more shocking than sticking a fork in a toaster.

Like I said, I'm ninety-nine percent sure that I know who did it—and that culprit is Seaview Rock's very own mayor, David Sturgess. I'm reserving the other one percent for reasonable doubt and the *very* slim chance I'm wrong. Unfortunately, Mayor McMurderer has an alibi that no one seems to want to question. What's worse is that it seems a few local business owners in town are also on his side; that is, the side that wants to keep Seaview Rock completely as-is.

Some people just can't handle change.

"Will?" Dennis asks flatly, holding up a basket of bright green tennis balls.

"Oh, uh, just put them on the shelf over there."

"Thanks."

Poor kid. Dennis is usually pretty chipper, but he's been speaking monosyllabically for the past two days, ever since he was released from jail where he was being held on suspicion of murder (see: dead tree farmer). He's not even wearing his trademark black skullcap, which I should be happy about because it's always been a minor annoyance to me, but without it, he doesn't quite look like Dennis.

Dennis only works for me part-time; he also writes a fairly popular web comic called *Bill Mulligan: Pet Shop Detective* that's loosely based on yours truly. The key difference is that Bill Mulligan gets to fight bad guys on rooftops and chase suspects down alleys and through seedy bars. The real-life Will Sullivan, meanwhile, takes a couple of ibuprofen because I gave myself a headache racking my brain, trying to conceive of some way to nail our dubious mayor for his crime.

Anyhow, *whoever* murdered the tree farmer did it in such a way that it mimicked the latest issue of *Bill Mulligan*, which made Dennis a suspect, which led to his arrest. A lack of physical evidence later led to his release, but ever since then he's been down in the dumps. Sarah and I have both tried to get him to talk about it, but he just shakes his head and insists he's fine.

If I had to guess, I'd say that it's not the being arrested part that bothers him as much as it is someone using his creativity to commit a murder; turning something he loves into something so heinous. I really feel for him, but I'm pretty bad at communicating any sort of condolences with people. I relate way better to animals.

"Dennis," I suggest, "why don't you go grab some lunch?"

"Not hungry." He continues to stack birdseed without turning.

"Okay… then how about you run down to Better Latte Than Never and grab us a couple of coffees?"

He pauses. "Sure."

"Take Spark with you. He could use some more leash training."

"Okay." Dennis unties his green apron and retrieves the blue leash hanging from a hook behind the counter. "Come on, Spark."

The little beige puggle leaps up from his place on his doggie bed and bounds toward the door. We've only had him for a few weeks, after adopting him from our local animal shelter, but he's a fast learner. It also helps having Rowdy around. Rowdy's our other pup, a terrier mix and another former shelter dog that I've had for a couple of years now and, if I'm being honest, he's smarter than most people. I think Ro's been training Spark just as much as I have.

Once the two of them are gone I glance around the empty store and sigh heavily. It's never truly quiet in the Pet Shop Stop— there are always parakeets chirping or cats meowing or pups playing in their kennels, but I prefer it that way. Silence is overrated.

The funny thing about all this, even if no one is laughing, is that things are going to change whether you like it or not. Take me, for instance: just a small handful of years ago I was married and owned a house and was happy. Then suddenly I wasn't anymore. Now I have Sarah, and the pet shop is doing great, and we're buying a place together. Even now, she's at our little rented house on Saltwater Drive, packing up the nonessentials while Dennis and I mind the store.

I've learned the hard way that things change, and if you don't adapt—roll with the punches, go with the flow, whatever you want to call it—you stagnate. You get left behind. You wither.

Apparently there are people in this town that think they can resist it and come out the other side okay. But like a rock in a stream, they can resist all they want and the only thing that's going to happen is everything around them will erode and get swept away.

And now I guess you're all caught up with what's going on in my life.

SUSIE GAYLE

CHAPTER 2

Bill Mulligan might get to carry a revolver and drink bourbon and do cool noir stuff, but Will Sullivan has one thing that good ol' Bill doesn't: several good friends that have his back.

And also a secret knock.

That night, after closing the shop, I head over to the Runside with Spark and Rowdy in tow. The Runside Bar & Grill is Seaview Rock's oldest establishment. It was originally barely more than a shack that served drinks to fishermen back when the town wasn't even a town. Now it's the best place around to get a steak or some fresh seafood and some home-brewed Whale of an Ale.

Rather, it's *usually* the best place around to get those things. But currently, it's closed.

I park in the rear and walk around to the front entrance. I look left and right and, seeing no one, I initiate the secret knock—two light raps in quick succession three times. *Tap-tap, tap-tap, tap-tap.*

A moment later the door opens and Sarah peers out. "Will, the door is unlocked."

"But we agreed on the secret knock."

She rolls her eyes. "No, *you* came up with the secret knock. No one else is doing that."

"Well, that's disappointing." The pups and I follow her inside to find everyone else already there. Holly, the tall, sable-haired owner of the Runside, stands at her usual place behind the bar. Mr. Casey, the elderly proprietor of Sockets & Sprockets, sits on a stool opposite her. Together, the three of them—Sarah, Holly, and Mr. Casey—comprise the Seaview Rock town council, the politically benevolent yin to the mayor's seemingly shady yang.

Also present is Sammy Barstow, my best friend and barber of going on two decades. And to my mild dismay, beside him is Karen Bear, my ex-wife and now-friend. Karen and I got past all the ugliness between us, but lately she and Sammy have been spending a lot of time together. I'd really like to believe them when they say they're just friends, but seeing them in proximity of each other as often as I have makes me think it might be more.

I know, I know, it's not my place to get between anyone. Still, it's a little weird and I don't care to be reminded of it, especially considering the nature of our secretive meeting.

"Hi everyone," I greet as I let Spark off the leash. The two pups immediately meander towards the empty tables, hoping some earlier diners might have dropped some morsels.

Holly slides a pint glass across the bar toward me. "Hey, Will. How's Dennis doing?"

I shrug a little. "He's… okay. How about you? Closing down early for our little gatherings can't be great for business."

She smiles with one side of her mouth. "There are more important things than money."

"Right," Sarah interjects, "which brings us to why we're here tonight. As we all know, Seaview Rock is divided." She positions herself behind the row of stools as she addresses us. I can't help but think how remarkable the change is between when we first met and now; once upon a time, Sarah was a somewhat reserved volunteer at the animal shelter and a part-time Pet Shop Stop employee. Now she's a co-owner, a councilwoman, and a natural leader.

"Those of us here represent one side," she continues. "And on this side, we want what's best for us and for the town, even if that means progressive action." We all know exactly what she's referring to; Seaview Rock has remained veritably unchanged since the mid-nineteenth century. The homes are mostly colonial style, the businesses are all mom-and-pop, and anything even remotely contemporary is met with disdain and usually squashed quickly, like a roach under a boot.

"The other side," she says, "seems to encompass those that are resistant to some of the changes that we want to bring about. The problem, of course, is that we don't know who's who. We know the mayor is involved. We know that a few business owners are on his side, including Sylvia Garner, who runs Better Latte Than Never, and Joe Miller."

"And don't forget the Blumbergs," I chime in. The Blumbergs are a couple of somewhat creepy old folks who are retired, but used to own a clothing store in the same storefront that currently houses the Pet Shop Stop. (I'm also pretty sure they laced cupcakes with rat poison and sent them to Sarah about a month ago.)

"Right," Sarah agrees, "which brings us to the real crux of the matter. Will has reason to believe that Mayor Sturgess is the one that murdered Logan Morse. Unfortunately, we have no evidence, and the police are not investigating him."

Sammy raises his hand politely.

Sarah rolls her eyes. "This isn't a classroom, Sam, you don't have to raise your hand."

"Do you think it's possible that the cops are in on this too?" he asks.

"No way," I cut in. "I've known Patty for years. We all have. I refuse to believe she could be involved." Patty Mayhew is our chief of police, and while she's capable of being a great friend, she's also made it clear that she's a cop first, always. "Moreover, I don't think the people on the mayor's side of things have any idea what he's done or that he was the one to do it. All they know is that someone killed Logan, and it was a convenient way out of their problem."

"Ha!" Mr. Casey says harshly. "Convenient, yeah. What are they, a bunch of ostriches with their heads in the sand? They'd have to be pretty stupid to believe that it wasn't one of their clique who did this."

"Ignorance is bliss," Holly mutters. "Will, didn't you tell us that Sylvia was hiding out in her house when Logan was killed?"

"That's right, and she told everyone she was out of town. They knew something was going to happen; they didn't want to be around when it did."

Sammy raises his hand again. Sarah pinches the bridge of her nose. "Sammy, just say whatever's on your mind."

"Okay. Why not us? We're all business owners in town. How do they form this sort of alliance and choose who gets in on it?"

"The mayor," I answer simply. "None of us advocated for him, much less voted for him. The people on his side are his constituency."

"And Seaview Rock has no term limit on mayor," Sarah adds. "He could stay in office until the day he dies if he continues to get reelected."

"So it's about control then," Mr. Casey grunts. "He wants to stay mayor, so to do that, he's going to do what he thinks he must to keep his people happy. And for them, that means keeping things the way they are."

Holly sighs. "So what can we do to make sure this doesn't happen again?"

"Well..." Sarah says slowly. "I think we would have to find a way to prove that the mayor killed Logan Morse. The others can't deny what's happening around them if Sturgess is convicted of murder."

"Easier said than done," I murmur. "I've been over it a thousand times in my head. There's no proof, and he has an alibi."

"What's his alibi?" Karen asks suddenly.

"His secretary claims that the mayor was in his office at town hall in the time frame that Morse was murdered," Sarah explains. "I mean, obviously he's lying to cover for the mayor, but—"

"Well, there's your way in," Karen says simply.

"What? Somehow get him to admit he was lying?" Sarah asks.

"Exactly." Karen pounds one tiny fist against her flat palm. Karen is a small woman—five-foot-three in heels—but she's fierce, and has a brash manner about her that some people find off-putting. I can't imagine why.

"No, Karen, we're not resorting to violence," Sarah insists. "That's what we're trying to *solve*."

"Wait a sec," I cut in. "She might be onto something." Sarah glances at me incredulously. "No, I don't mean beat the guy up," I assure her. "But maybe put the squeeze on him a little. Let him know that we know what happened and that he was lying—maybe even pretend that we have some sort of evidence. How willing could he be to go to jail for Sturgess?"

Mr. Casey shakes his head. "He's already in it. No way he'll backpedal now."

"I have another idea," Sarah tells us. "I've been thinking about it a lot these last couple of days. What if we try to push something big through the town council? It would have to be something we know they'll be against; it could be leasing public land to a fast-food chain or hiring some postmodern architect to renovate town hall. They'll try something; they've already come so close to messing up. This time, we'll be ready for them and catch them in the act."

"No way," I say immediately. "You're talking about putting yourself in immediate danger." After all, we are talking about people that sent Sarah poisoned cupcakes and another that murdered a man just for the threat of selling his land to a corporation.

"I like it," Mr. Casey says.

"Hush," I scold him.

"I agree with Will," Karen pipes up. "It's a dumb plan. You'd be painting a target on your own back."

"Thank you, Karen," I tell her. To Sarah, I say, "Just give me a day or so to talk to the secretary. They're the ones acting out of desperation; our moves need to be calculated. We need to think this through. We may only get one chance, and I'd prefer it be one that doesn't, you know, get any of us killed."

"Or even hurt," Holly adds.

Sarah's nostrils flare a little, but she relents. "Fine. I'll give you one day."

CHAPTER 3

The ride home is mostly silent. Sarah stares out the passenger-side window of my SUV while the two pups lie in the back seat across a blanket.

"It's not dumb," she mutters finally.

"I never said your plan was dumb," I protest. "Karen did. But I do think it's dangerous. These people have already shown a capacity to do awful things—"

"Stop saying 'these people,'" she insists. "I refuse to believe that people like Sylvia and Joe are evil. We know Sturgess is a monster, and those Blumbergs are off their rockers, but I don't want this to tear the town apart any further. I have a responsibility to do what's best for everyone in town, not just the people I like."

"I understand, but I don't think that putting yourself at an unnecessary risk is the answer. I really think—"

My cell phone rings from the center console, cutting me off. I glance at it and groan. "It's Strauss."

"Aren't you going to answer it?"

Honestly, I was going to ignore it, but instead I roll my eyes and answer. "Hi, Georgia."

"Will, can you meet me tomorrow?" she asks curtly.

"Actually, I've kind of got some stuff going on—"

"Don't we all? Meet me at the park behind the pet shop at eleven." She hangs up.

I scoff. "Sure Georgia, always nice to chat with you."

*   *   *

The next morning, I open the Pet Shop Stop at eight a.m. Sarah stays behind to get some more packing done at the house. Dennis comes in around nine, his mousy brown hair sticking up in tufts. Poor guy doesn't look like he's been sleeping much lately.

At ten-thirty Sarah comes in to relieve me so that I can go meet Strauss. Before I head down to the park, I ask Dennis for a favor.

"Listen," I tell him, "I know this whole… thing has got you a little twisted up. But I could really use your help."

"Sure, Will," he replies, monotone.

"Dennis," I lower my voice conspiratorially. "I don't think you understand. I could really use your *help*."

For a moment, his eyes light up. "You mean with an investigation?" he whispers.

I nod solemnly. "I'm trying to find the man who killed Logan Morse."

"I'm in," he says immediately. "Whatever you need."

"Good. I want you to head down to town hall. There's a young guy that works there, about your height with black hair. He drives a red coupe. He's going to leave for lunch within the hour. When he does, I want you to follow him, and then call me and tell me where he goes." Thanks to Sammy, I know at least a few details about the mayor's secretary, and having Dennis case the joint—to use some Bill Mulligan parlance—gives me the time I need to meet with Georgia Strauss.

"You got it," he tells me, a sudden verve in his demeanor. I figured he'd want to help out if he could, all things considered.

After Dennis leaves, I call for Rowdy and the two of us walk the couple of blocks to the small park down the road. When we arrive, Strauss is already there, sitting on a bench and seemingly watching the birds peck at worms in the grass.

I sit down beside her as Rowdy chases the birds away. "So, I'm here."

"Thank you for meeting me." Strauss is a county judge that lives on the hill in Seaview Rock—not a literal hill, that's just what we locals call the ritzy part of town. I'd peg her around late fifties, with short silver hair, piercing eyes and a sharp nose, all of which lend to her resemblance to a hawk.

And I've also found that she has a habit of being annoyingly cryptic, ever since she's been hiring me on for private cases.

"I have something for you," she says in her typical curt manner.

"I can't. I'm still suspended," I reply. "Unless you managed to get me out of that." Just a few days ago, Patty Mayhew found out that I was investigating Morse's murder after she explicitly told me not to. Patty spoke with her friends in the state police and got my PI license suspended for sixty days as a warning.

"I'm still working on that. But this isn't an investigation. Let's call it… research."

I chuckle a little. "And what would Patty call it?"

"I couldn't say. But if you're that concerned, then my advice would be don't get caught."

"Great. Do you want to tell me what it is before I tell you no?"

"Scones," she says simply.

"Scones?"

She nods. "There used to be a place here in Seaview Rock called Buddy's Bakery. You remember it?"

"Vaguely."

"They had, hands-down, the most delicious scones I've ever tasted. Sadly, they closed suddenly about twenty years ago—no, eighteen, actually."

Eighteen years ago I was in my early twenties and away at college, which would explain why Buddy's Bakery doesn't ring many bells with me. "Great. What does this have to do with me?"

"I'd like you to find out what happened to those scones."

I rub my temples. "You have got to be kidding me."

She looks over at me for the first time, and I find it hard to hold her piercing gaze. "I assure you, Will, I am not kidding. Losing those scones was one of the single biggest regrets of my life."

"I don't have time for this." I stand up, growing angry. "We both know this isn't about scones, just like your 'dog-napping spree' wasn't about missing dogs. Can you just try not to be cryptic and weird for one minute and just tell me what this is really about?"

She stands too, sliding the strap of her designer handbag up onto her shoulder. "I'm sorry I can't give you more to go on, but I have every confidence in your ability. I'll make it worth your while; time and a half your usual rate." She glances over at Rowdy, happily chasing birds away. "Find out what happened to those scones, Will. I'll be waiting for your call." She strides off, leaving me dumbfounded and annoyed.

CHAPTER 4

Dennis calls me as I'm heading back to the Pet Shop Stop from my meeting with Strauss.

"That guy you asked me to follow? He just went into the Chinese take-out place downtown."

"You mean Wok N' Roll?" I ask him.

"No the other one. Wok This Way."

"Got it. Thanks, Dennis." I hang up and, instead of heading back into the pet shop, I get into my SUV with Rowdy in the passenger seat and drive the several blocks to the Chinese food restaurant. As I head over there, I consider how exactly I'm going to confront the secretary without scaring him off or making him suspicious. I think the best course of action is to just play aloof— pretend I recognize him from elsewhere and get the guy talking about the murder, tell him there are rumors around town. I can read people pretty well, and hopefully the way he reacts will give me something to go on.

"Stay here, pal," I tell Rowdy as I pull up in front of Wok This Way. I get out and stride quickly to the door, but before I can pull it open someone pushes it from the inside and I suddenly find myself face to face with the mayor's secretary—a young guy, black haired and clean shaven, in a tie and shirt with the sleeves rolled up to his elbows.

"Oh, excuse me." I go left, and so does he. I go right, and he does too. He rolls his eyes in annoyance and steps aside for me to enter.

"Hey, um, don't I know you from somewhere?" I ask him. "Aren't you the mayor's secretary?"

"Assistant," he grumbles.

"Gesundheit."

"No, I'm the mayor's assistant, not his secretary."

"Right, right. You're, uh…" I snap my fingers as if I'm trying to recall a name.

"Aaron," he tells me. "Aaron Sutherland."

"Right! Aaron. Yes. My girlfriend is on the town council. She speaks very highly of—"

Aaron Sutherland scoffs. "I know who you are, Mr. Sullivan. And I saw your employee follow me here. He couldn't be more conspicuous if he was in a police car with the sirens on."

"…Oh." Well, so much for best intentions.

"What do you want?" he asks, narrowing his eyes.

I back away from the door and he steps outside too, joining me on the sidewalk. The guy is clearly smarter than I gave him credit for, and it's possible that Sturgess warned him about me and my penchant for getting involved in things.

I guess I might as well tell him what's on my mind.

"Look, Aaron," I start, "we both know that the mayor wasn't in his office the morning Logan Morse was killed. But you told the cops he was. Now, I'm not a lawyer, but I'm pretty sure that's a felony. What would that be—aiding and abetting at worst, obstruction of justice at best?"

Aaron stares me down evenly. "And what would the police think if they knew that we were having this conversation right now, Mr. Sullivan?"

Well. I guess Mayor Sturgess is aware of my suspension. But there's no way I can back down now. "I would assume they'd be unhappy, but probably far less concerned with me than our mayor having committed a murder."

Aaron shrugs a little. "The police questioned Mayor Sturgess. They found no reason to suspect him. If you're so sure, where's your proof?"

Inside I'm growing increasingly irritated with how smug this guy is, but outwardly I force a smirk and tell him, "Oh, don't worry about that. It'll all come to light very soon."

For just a split second, I see the guy get nervous. His eyes widen and his gaze flits to the left. But then he shakes his head and says, "No. If you had anything you would've gone straight to the cops. We wouldn't even be having this conversation."

Now it's my turn to shrug smugly. "Maybe. Or maybe I want to give him an opportunity. Seaview Rock doesn't need another scandal and he knows it. He can do the honorable thing, turn himself in and confess, or the cops will come for him, and I'll make sure there's lots of press around when they do. I'll give him until tomorrow afternoon to make a choice."

Aaron narrows his eyes again, scrutinizing me, as if trying to determine if I'm lying or not. Then without another word he turns and strides to his car.

I let out a long sigh as Dennis trots up behind me. "Hey," he asks breathlessly, "how'd that go?"

"Not great. I told him I suspect the mayor of murder and that I have evidence proving it."

"The mayor?!" Dennis balks. "You think the mayor did this?"

"I know he did it."

"Then why not just hand the evidence over to the cops?" he asks.

"Because I don't actually have any, Dennis. And now I have just over twenty-four hours to get my hands on some."

He frowns. "So you don't actually have evidence, and you told him all that? You know he'll just go back to the mayor and tell him, right?"

"I'm counting on it." Dennis is right; chances are good that Aaron will run back to Sturgess and tell him about our little encounter. And if there is any evidence to be had, Sturgess will probably make a desperate attempt to cover it up.

"I need you to go back to town hall and keep an eye out," I tell Dennis. "If you see the mayor or his assistant go anywhere, call me. Sammy or myself will come relieve you in a couple hours."

"Sure thing."

"And Dennis? Be discreet. This isn't *Bill Mulligan*. We may only get one chance at this, and we need to make it count."

"You got it, Will. I'll be like a shadow. Like a ninja. Like a... like a..."

"I get the idea."

Dennis trots back over to his car as I head toward my own. Just as I'm opening my door, I get that strange prickly-back-of-the-neck sensation you get when you think you're being watched.

I turn and glance across the street to see Patty Mayhew, in her police uniform, sitting in her cruiser at the curb. Her eyes are hidden behind a pair of aviator sunglasses but I'm certain she's looking right at me.

She nods to me, just once. I can't tell if it's a friendly gesture or a warning. I nod back slightly and then get in my car.

SUSIE GAYLE

CHAPTER 5

I head back to the Pet Shop Stop to share my "meeting" with Aaron Sutherland with Sarah. I know she's not going to be thrilled about me involving her brother in an investigation again—especially an investigation that I'm not even supposed to be doing—but you know what they say about desperate times.

When I arrive back at the shop, Rowdy and I are greeted by not only Spark, but also by a peppy little white-and-black cockapoo—one of our kennel pups (I have a real problem with calling them "inventory"). Sarah is on her hands and knees, the top half of her in the dog's kennel as she scrubs the floor.

"What's all this?" I ask. "Did someone have an accident?"

"Like you wouldn't believe." She grimaces.

"Need some help?"

"Nope, I got it. What did Strauss want?"

Right, that. I'm going to have to start tying strings around my fingers to remind myself of all the things I'm supposed to be looking into at any given time.

"She, uh… well, she's strange. She wants me to 'research' a bakery that closed down some years ago here in town."

"Oh?" Sarah straightens and tugs the yellow rubber gloves off her hands. "I don't remember a bakery here."

"I think it closed before you moved here—we're going back about eighteen years. It was called Buddy's Bakery."

"And what's the significance?"

I shrug. "I can never tell with Strauss, and she can never just tell me. Figured I'd start by poking around online."

"Eighteen years… that would have been late nineties. You can try, but I wouldn't expect it to yield much." She corrals the little cockapoo back into her kennel as I go around the counter to use the computer we keep there. "By the way, did you make any headway with the mayor's secretary?"

"Assistant."

"Bless you."

"No, it's the mayor's assistant, not secretary." I click on the little icon to open the internet, but then I notice that there's another window open. I click on it; it's a word-processing document with about a page of text typed out.

"Fine, 'assistant.' Did you talk with him?"

"Yeah…" I say absentmindedly as I scan the document. "Sarah, what's this?"

"What's what?"

"This document on the computer."

"Oh. I, uh…" She clears her throat. "I thought I'd closed that."

"Uh-huh. Because you wouldn't want me to see your proposition to…" I look up at her. "Renovate Dalton Manor into a contemporary art gallery?"

She looks away. "You know it's not real. It's just to…"

"To paint a target on your back." I shake my head, dismayed. "I thought you were going to give me time."

"And I am," she insists. "That's just a precaution—"

"What, in case I fail?"

"No, Will, it's because…" She shrugs. "I'm sorry. I just think my plan is better than yours."

"Your plan is going to get someone hurt. Probably you!" I almost shout.

She bristles. "Well, did you ever stop to consider that your plan might get *you* hurt?" she fires back. "I don't want that!"

"I'm not going to get hurt—"

"Will, we're dealing with at least one person who seems to have no problem murdering a lifelong friend. Do you think he would have any trouble getting rid of you?"

"I…" I guess I hadn't really thought of it that way. "Even so, that doesn't matter. Better me than you."

"No, it's not!" She throws her hands up in frustration and one yellow rubber glove goes flying. "*I'm* the one that upset everybody. *I'm* the one that's been pushing all these new ideas that they're so afraid of. *I'm* the one that created the loophole that got

Logan Morse killed." Her arms fall to her sides and her shoulders droop in defeat. "This is all my fault."

I come around the counter and hug her tightly. "No, it's not. You can't think like that. Everything you've done has been in the name of improving things around here for everyone. You're no more to blame than Dennis is for writing a comic. It's the people that took those ideas and twisted them into something ugly that are to blame here."

She hugs me back, resting her head on my shoulder, and says, "I'm sorry, Will, but there's nothing you can say that's going to stop me."

"Please…"

"I'm calling an emergency council meeting tomorrow night. I'm going to introduce the new proposal then. You know Holly and Mr. Casey will approve it."

"Don't."

"It'll work. I know it will." She lets me go and wipes her eyes. "I'm going for a walk." She strides toward the door without looking back.

At the mention of the word "walk" Rowdy leaps up and follows her out. A moment later they're both gone.

CHAPTER 6

"Hey pal, is this a bad time?" Sammy asks as he enters the store, finding me sitting on the floor with my back to the counter and my chin in my hands.

"No, it's fine." If I'm being honest, I was contemplating ways that I could potentially prevent Sarah from calling an emergency meeting. The only ideas I have so far are to tie her to a chair for the next day or so, or to burn town hall to the ground so that council has nowhere to meet—neither of which are terribly viable options.

"You want to talk about it?" he asks as I stand and straighten my green apron.

"Not really." No matter how stubborn Sarah is being, the last thing she needs right now is to alienate any friends. "What's up, Sammy?"

"Oh, I was just in the neighborhood, figured I'd drop in on you…"

"I can always tell when you're lying, Sam."

"Okay, you got me." He shrugs. "I saw Sarah storm past the barbershop a few minutes ago, still wearing her pet shop apron. You guys alright?"

"Eh, just a little spat." If Sammy can tell when I'm lying, he doesn't let on.

"Good."

I look over at him with an eyebrow raised. "Good?"

"Yeah. You two have been together for a while now. I don't think I've ever seen you argue. It's healthy."

Sheesh, if he only knew just how not healthy the nature of our argument really was… but I understand he's trying to be a good friend. "You're right."

"So, any luck with the mayor's secretary?" he asks.

"Assistant."

"Salud."

"No, I mean he's the mayor's assistant, not his secretary." I quickly tell Sammy about my encounter with Aaron Sutherland and my on-the-fly plan. "I've got Dennis keeping an eye on town hall; if the mayor goes anywhere, he's going to let me know."

"Sounds good. Anything I can do to help?"

"Not at the moment, but I'll let you know… Oh, you know what? There actually is. Do you remember a place here in town called Buddy's Bakery, closed down about eighteen years ago?"

"Yeah, I vaguely remember. Why, what about it?"

"Any idea why it closed?"

Sammy strokes his chin and sighs. "Jeez, that's going back a long way. If I recall correctly, Buddy—that was the owner—"

"I got that, yeah."

"Well, Buddy wasn't native. He moved here from god-knows-where and opened up a bakery. He was only here for a couple of years at best. Man, now that you mention it, I remember that place having the best scones. I mean, they were really good. Moist and delicious, not like those flaky, dry things they serve up at Better Latte Than Never."

I roll my eyes. "So I've heard."

"No, I mean these things were incredible. There was probably a stick of butter in each one, but if you took one bite you wouldn't care—"

"Sammy."

"Sorry. Uh, where was I?"

"Buddy wasn't here long…"

"Right. Buddy wasn't here long. If memory serves me, he wasn't exactly popular around town."

"Why was that?"

Sammy smirks. "Will, I would've been around twenty-three or twenty-four at the time, which means I was a lot more concerned with cars and girls than in-town politics. Plus that's around the time I was getting ready to take over the barbershop. All I remember for sure is that Buddy wasn't well liked."

"So what happened?"

"I don't know. One day the bakery was just closed. No explanation; no note. He defaulted on the lease; left all the equipment behind and everything. Just… left it all." Sammy shrugs. "I guess he just couldn't handle being a pariah."

"What about family? Did he have any around here? Was Buddy his real name? Where did he move here from?"

Sammy holds up both hands. "Whoa, hey. Like I said, I didn't really know that much back then, and I remember even less of it now. If you really want to know, you'd be better off asking one of the older folks around here—maybe Mr. Casey would know better than me." Even though there's no one else around, he lowers his voice and asks, "Why do you want to know all this? Is this relevant to the case somehow?"

"I don't know yet," I tell him. "But I have a feeling it might—"

My cell phone rings, cutting me off mid-sentence as it seems to like to do.

"Hey, Dennis."

"Will. Mayor Sturgess is on the move; he just got into his car and he looks kind of nervous."

"Yeah, I'm sure he's looking for me. Or you. Follow him, but be careful. Stay a few car lengths away and don't run any lights. Just don't lose him, either." Listen to me, acting like I know what I'm talking about. I've only ever chased one person in a car, an alleged dog-napper, and apparently I was as conspicuous as Dennis was earlier.

"Okay. Remember that GPS thing I showed you?" Dennis asks. "Use that to find me."

"See you soon." I hang up before I realize that I have no one to watch the store while I'm gone, and I'm not even sure that Sarah has her keys with her. "Sammy... could you...?"

"Say no more." He holds up a hand to indicate it's no problem. "Just don't be all day."

"I won't. Thanks. You're the best!" I yank off my apron, grab my keys, and dash out the door.

CHAPTER 7

D ennis is pretty tech-savvy. He's not like a professional hacker or some ridiculous thing like you'd see in the movies, but he certainly knows his way around almost anything digital. Even knowing half of what he knows would put you leagues beyond me, who just learned this past year that I can access the internet on my phone.

Recently Dennis showed me how I can find people using my GPS app, but only if they allow me to. Dennis used himself as an example to show me, and never removed it, so if I want to I can tell where he is at pretty much any given time—which, it turns out, comes in handy when you ask your girlfriend's little brother to track a murderer for you.

I prop my phone in the center console of my SUV and turn on the GPS app, and then set it to follow the little blue dot that represents Dennis (or rather, Dennis's phone). Annoyingly, his dot keeps moving as mine tries to catch up, and the thing keeps rerouting me around blocks and up side streets as it tries to ascertain his position.

Finally, after about ten minutes, his dot ceases its slow trek across the map and sits still. I don't recognize his position on the little digital display—never was any good at reading maps—but as I get closer, I realize that I know exactly where Mayor Sturgess went.

At the southern edge of Seaview Rock, less than a quarter mile from the border of town, my GPS tells me to hang a right onto a tiny gravel access road that cuts into the forest that stretches from there into the neighboring borough. About forty yards down the access road is a black sedan, parked lengthwise across the gravel.

Dennis stands behind the car, just outside the passenger door, his elbows propped up on the roof and a pair of binoculars to his eyes. He doesn't lower them, even as I park and get out to join him.

"You have binoculars?" I ask.

"You don't?" Now he lowers them and frowns. "You're the investigator here. You should have a good pair of binoculars." He passes them over to me. "Here, take a look."

The reason I recognize this place is because where we are, this stretch of forest, is right across the street from Morse's tree farm—the very same land that the now-deceased Logan Morse wanted to sell to Sprawl-Mart in a seven-figure deal. The very same reason he was murdered.

I prop my elbows on the roof of the car and take a look for myself. From Dennis's vantage point, I can clearly see the eastern section of the property, where the Morse farmhouse stands.

Sure enough, in the driveway is the mayor's silver luxury vehicle. Beyond it is the porch of the farmhouse, where just last week I witnessed Logan's son Kyle threaten two Sprawl-Mart executives with a shotgun.

Currently, however, Mayor Sturgess is on that porch, pacing back and forth as his mouth moves a mile a minute, ranting. His salt-and-pepper hair looks mussed and he's taken off his tie, if he was wearing one. Kyle Morse, a tall, strong-looking kid in his late twenties with shaggy brown hair, leans against the house with his arms folded across his chest, appearing thoroughly annoyed.

"Well, would you look at that," I murmur.

"What does it mean?" Dennis asks.

"I'm not entirely sure, but I find it awfully peculiar that after talking with his assistant, our friend the mayor runs straight to the Morse farm."

After his father was found murdered at the Runside, I had gone to speak with Kyle myself, and now, as I watch the mayor losing his cool on that same porch, I try to recall as much of the conversation as I can.

I had introduced myself as a local business owner in town. Kyle told me other business owners had come; they wanted to see if Kyle would take the Sprawl-Mart deal now that his father was dead. But Kyle turned it down—a million dollars, maybe more, for six and a half acres of Seaview Rock.

Then he had told me that he was convinced that his father, Logan, had run his mouth off to the wrong people around town and gotten himself killed. And I had discounted him as a suspect, because…

"Oh my god," I murmur as I lower the binoculars. "He's part of it."

"Who? The young guy?" Dennis asks.

I nod. "I think so. See, when I talked to him before, I thought he couldn't have been involved because he didn't sign the deal— and that meant he didn't want the money. But of course he didn't want the money. He's in on it. He's with *them*."

"Who's 'them'?"

I just shake my head; it's a bit too much to explain to Dennis at the moment. Kyle thought that I was among his "side," with the likes of Sylvia Garner and Joe Miller, who owns the grocery store in town. And the mayor.

"He knows darn well that the mayor killed his father. He might have even helped him do it."

"Will, are you sure?" Dennis asks.

"Of course not. If I've learned anything in the past week, it's that even the right guess isn't right until you can prove it. So I'm going to prove it."

"How?"

"…I have no idea." I glance through the binoculars again to see Sturgess retreat down the porch, the younger Morse watching him go. The mayor opens his car door, smoothes his hair, and reties his tie. As he backs down the driveway, we both duck down behind

Dennis's car; it's not likely that he can see us from the road, but we can't afford to take that chance.

"What's next?" Dennis asks in a half-whisper, crouched down beside me in the gravel.

"I'm going to see if Mr. Mayor heads back to his office or not," I tell him. "Do you mind hanging out here for a little while and seeing if Kyle Morse goes anywhere?"

"No problem," he says, dangling the binoculars from his wrist by the strap. "When I'm done here, you should have these."

"What? No, they're yours."

"Consider them a gift. They might come in handy, considering your line of work."

"Thanks." I smirk. "You know, you're getting pretty decent at this whole subterfuge thing."

"Subterfuge?"

"Discretion? Intrigue? Guile?"

"Ah. Thanks. I just ask myself, 'What would Bill Mulligan do?' And then do the opposite." He smiles sheepishly.

"Good. Keep it up, and keep me in the loop."

CHAPTER 8

I lose sight of the mayor's car as I head back into town, so I go straight to town hall and park across the street at a meter, watching the lot.

It all makes sense, and I scold myself for not considering it earlier. I assumed originally that it was about the money, but Kyle Morse told me himself that he thought his father was foolish for wanting to sell the land. He loves his farm and he loves Seaview Rock, and with his dear old dad out of the way, everything would go to him, since Logan's wife passed away a few years earlier.

I guess I'm going to have to change my slogan of "it's always about the money" to "it's usually about the money." Some people just want to keep things the same.

Sturgess's car pulls into the parking lot about a minute after I arrive. He sits in the car for a long moment, but his windows are too tinted for me to see what he's doing. When he gets out, he stuffs his cell phone in the pocket of his trousers; he was on the phone. He paces back and forth next to his car a few times, every now and then glancing up expectedly.

A couple minutes later, an ancient pickup truck pulls in and parks a few spaces away from him. An elderly man in overalls and a green baseball cap gets out slowly. I shudder a little as I recognize him—John Blumberg, retiree and former owner of Blumberg's clothing store downtown, where the Pet Shop Stop is currently.

Mr. Blumberg and the mayor exchange a few words, and then they head into town hall together, no doubt to collude on how best to avoid further scrutiny. The Blumbergs are a shady couple of old folks, and as I mentioned, I'm pretty sure they were the ones that sent Sarah a batch of cyanide-laced cupcakes in the hopes that she would share them with town council, and possibly me.

What the Blumbergs' involvement in this is, I don't know, but I have no doubt that they're in on it. Oh, to be a fly on that wall.

Wait a second.

Light bulb.

"I don't necessarily have to get evidence against him," I murmur to myself, "if there was a way to get a confession from someone." After all, there might not be any evidence to be found; it seems like the mayor covered his tracks pretty well. His biggest weakness right now is the number of people that know about what he's done—at least Kyle Morse and Mr. Blumberg, likely his assistant, Aaron Sutherland, and possibly others.

Getting any one of them to spill the beans would at least put him under a magnifying glass as far as the cops are concerned—

"Eep!" I gasp a little as someone knocks on my passenger side window. I glance over and my stomach ties itself into a knot;

Patty Mayhew stands outside my SUV, peering in at me in a manner that is anything but friendly.

I roll the window all the way down. Patty leans both elbows on the door frame and gives me a look like a parent who caught a child with their hand in the cookie jar.

"What are you doing, Will?"

"Nothing." I shrug. That's me, the excuse expert. "Just, uh, waiting for Sarah."

"Oh? And where's Sarah?" she asks casually.

"She… is… in town hall."

"Yeah? Right now?"

"Uh-huh."

"That's odd." Patty sniffs and adds, "I just saw her walking past Miller's with your dog."

"Really? Weird. I guess she decided to walk back to the pet shop." I almost cringe at how bad I am at playing dumb.

"I suppose that means you should probably get back there too, huh?" she asks.

"Well, I would, but I've got some errands to run, and—"

"Cut the bull, Will," she says suddenly, her tone growing harsh. "I told you once before that I didn't want you investigating the mayor, and here you are, outside town hall at the same time that he comes back. If I didn't know any better, I'd say you were keeping an eye on him."

"I don't know what you're—"

"What's more," she says loudly over me, "I hear from my friends in the state police that someone is trying to overturn your suspension. I've always considered us friends, Will, but I don't like my friends sneaking around behind my back, and I *really* don't like my authority being called into question. That makes me angry, and you have yet to truly see my bad side."

I say nothing as she adjusts her flat-brimmed hat and lets out a long sigh through flared nostrils. "Now, there's only one other person in this whole town that I know of who could overturn that. I don't know how she's involved in anything at all here, but you could save me a lot of time and hassle if you just tell me the truth right now."

I close my eyes and shake my head. I can't give up Strauss. Or rather, I *shouldn't* give up Strauss… but then again, why not? Patty has done me favors in the past. She's overlooked all the times I got involved in things I shouldn't have. There are several times she's been a friend to me. But Strauss? Sure, she pays me. But that doesn't mean I'm beholden to her in any way. Besides, she's cryptic and odd and I'm not really sure what her endgame is in all this.

Also, Patty has handcuffs on her belt and access to a cell and would have every reason to throw me in one for twenty-four hours, which might mean I never get my chance to bring Sturgess to justice.

"Alright, fine. You want the truth?"

"Nothing but," Patty replies.

"Okay. I am absolutely convinced that the mayor killed Logan Morse. I think that he did it to keep certain people happy, people that will make sure that he gets reelected. I think that Kyle Morse is in on it, and that the Blumbergs are too. Yes, I'm investigating it. Yes, Georgia Strauss is the one that's working to get my suspension overturned. Yes, I'm investigating something for her too, but it's not related. And..."

Oh. There goes another light bulb.

I rub my face with both hands. "And you already know all this because the mayor's assistant told him, and he told you. You already know what I'm doing."

She nods slowly.

"Patty, please tell me you're not involved too."

"Will, I want you to roll up this window and step out of the car."

"Patty..."

"I'm *not* going to ask twice."

I do what she asks. I roll up my window and get out. Then, right there on Main Street, in full view of town hall and everyone out and about, I do as I'm told and put my hands on the roof of the car as Patty reads me my rights and arrests me.

CHAPTER 9

The drive to the police station is only a few blocks, so my experience handcuffed in the back of a cruiser is brief. Patty says nothing the entire time, and neither do I. At one point my cell phone goes off in my pocket, but I couldn't reach it with my hands behind my back even if I wanted to.

She pulls up to the station, opens my door, and takes me by an arm up the concrete steps and inside. The officer behind the front desk, Tom, looks up in surprise. I've always liked Tom; he's a fairly quiet guy, pleasant enough, and he's helped me out on a couple occasions as well. He must know why I'm here, though, because he shakes his head slightly in dismay.

Patty leads me to a small boxy room with no windows at the rear of the station. The only contents are a small square table and two plastic chairs.

Then she does two things I don't expect at all. First, she drags a chair to the corner of the room, stands on it, and tugs two wires from the back of the camera mounted in the corner.

Second, she takes the cuffs off of me.

"Sit."

I do.

"I'm sorry about all that," she says, "but it was necessary. It had to be public. There's a good chance that at least a couple of people at town hall saw, so I'm sure the mayor will catch wind of it."

"You… you did that so people would see?"

She nods.

"I don't understand."

Patty pulls the plastic chair over to the table, sits, and folds her hands before she says, "I believe you."

"You do?"

"I do now. I didn't at first, or else I never would've suspended your license. I thought there was no way the mayor could be involved, or that there was some sort of conspiracy going on. I haven't been sitting on my hands, Will; I've been investigating Morse's murder as well. But there's nothing to be found, not a scrap of evidence, not even a decent lead. And then I had a visitor."

"Who?"

"Sylvia Garner, the owner of Better Latte Than Never. She came to see me; she was spooked. She started to tell me… something. She said that it was never supposed to go this far. That they didn't know what they'd do. Then she changed her mind and ran out of here."

Shortly after Logan Morse's murder, I had gone to see Sylvia at the request of Strauss. Sylvia had told her employees that she was going to be out of town for a couple of days, but really she was hiding out at home. She knew that something was going to happen to Logan, but (I hope) she didn't know what. Either way, she assumed she'd need an alibi.

"That's all she said? 'They didn't know what they'd do'?" I ask.

"That's all she said."

"Then why not start calling people in for questioning?" I insist. "The mayor's assistant, the Blumbergs, Sylvia… get someone to talk."

Patty shakes her head. "It's not that easy, Will. Right now, the mayor and his people think the law is on his side. I'm sure within a few hours everyone's going to know that I arrested you, so they'll continue to believe that I don't suspect him. If I start bringing people in and no one talks, I've got nothing. They know you're onto them, and they got nervous; hopefully now that I've 'arrested' you, they'll relax a little. That gives us an advantage."

"So it's 'us' now?"

"Not officially. Not on paper and not in public. Heck, not even outside this room. I don't want to see or hear from you again until you bring me something solid. But I'll keep working on my end too. Hopefully, together we can make sure that things like this never happen again."

"Things?" I ask. "As in, more than one?"

She sighs. "It wasn't a coincidence that I ran into you outside of town hall. I was already there, doing some digging. You haven't seen what I've seen; you don't know what I know. Like most people, before you started getting involved in stuff like this, you kept to yourself, right? Just lived your life, ran your business. You didn't get involved in local politics or care much what happened, as long as you could keep doing what you were doing."

She's right. Before I saw my first body, I minded my own business. I wasn't a shut-in or a hermit or anything like that, but I didn't really get involved outside of my little pet shop microcosm.

"What do you mean, I don't know what you know?"

Patty shifts in her chair. "Remember your pal Derik Dobson?"

I scoff. "Dobson, yeah. I remember." Derik Dobson was the CEO of a chain of pet stores called Pet Emporium. About six years ago now, he offered to buy my shop and turn it into one of his locations. I refused, of course. Then about three years ago, he purchased an old warehouse in town with the intention of opening a huge store here, which would have put me out of business.

He never got the chance, though, on account of being murdered by Sharon Estes, a local real estate agent who had a sordid history with Dobson. It was the first murder I'd ever been privy to.

"Wait," I say, thinking out loud, "you believe that Dobson's murder was part of this?" I shake my head. "Sharon killed him because of what he did to her."

"Sure, that's what she told you. And maybe it's true. But Sharon Estes was on the town council, and she was one of Seaview Rock's biggest proponents of maintaining our historic value.

Keeping things status quo." Patty leans forward and asks, "Do you really think it was just circumstance that led him here, and that he worked with her? Doesn't that seem just a little fortuitous?"

"I... I guess I never really thought about it like that."

"It's not just Morse, and it's not just Dobson—although those are the only two I know of that were killed for what they were trying to do. Go back a few decades, and you'll see that every couple of years or so, someone gets the bright idea to try to change things around here. But every time, those people seem to back down, change their minds, or leave town suddenly. And in a couple cases, they just... vanish."

"Buddy," I murmur.

"What's that?" she asks, an eyebrow raised.

"Buddy's Bakery," I tell her. "The owner, Buddy, he left town suddenly one night."

"You remember that?"

"No. It's what Strauss asked me to look into."

"Hm." Patty eases back in the chair. "That was one of the very first cases I ever handled—sort of. Back then I was an officer-in-training, fresh out of the academy. I remember that one morning the bakery just didn't open. No one had heard anything from Buddy. A day went by, then another, and then another before the police chief asked me to swing by his house, see what was up. His truck was gone, and so was a lot of his stuff. But he left behind his furniture, appliances—looked like he took whatever would fit in his truck and just left." She shakes her head. "Everyone else took it at face value, just like we did with Dobson. They all just shrugged and said, 'Good riddance.' But it never did sit right with me that someone would up and leave like that. There had to be a reason."

"Yeah," I agree. "There had to be a reason." Just like there has to be a reason that Strauss asked me to look into Buddy's sudden disappearance. And after everything that Patty just told me, I highly doubt that Morse's murder and Buddy's Bakery are unrelated.

"I need to go talk to some people," I tell her. "Assuming I'm free to go, that is."

"Yeah, go. But if anyone asks, I let you off with a warning. Whatever you do, don't make them have to call me again."

I nod. "Thanks, Patty."

CHAPTER 10

I head outside and walk the several blocks back to my car, where Patty arrested me. As I walk I pull out my cell phone and notice that I have a missed call and a text message from Dennis: *No movement from Morse. Should I stay?*

I call him back. "Thanks for all your help, Dennis. Can you head back to the pet shop and relieve Sammy? He's watching the place while I, uh, look into some stuff."

"Sure, Will. No problem."

"Thanks. I'll be in touch." After I hang up with Dennis, I try to call Sarah but it rings four times and then goes to voicemail. I don't know where she's gone or what she's doing, but at least I know that Rowdy is with her, which means she's safe.

Then I head over to Sockets & Sprockets to see Mr. Casey.

Barton Casey's family has had roots in Seaview Rock since before the town even had a name. One of his ancestors helped open the first fish hatchery here and was partially responsible for the boom into what is our present-day town. Eventually they sold their shares, and these days they own and operate a gas station, the auto body shop, and a few other local businesses. Mr. Casey, or "the old man," as he's called around here, only runs Sockets & Sprockets; he leaves the other business interests to his children.

I pull into a parking space and head inside to the small customer waiting area. It's a nice day, so the three garage bay doors are open and the sounds of socket wrenches and pneumatic tools fill the air.

The receptionist, Brenda, knows me, so I smile politely and point to the closed door of the rear office. She nods and I head inside.

Mr. Casey sits behind his deck, hunting and pecking at a computer keyboard and squinting at the screen. He's around seventy, just about completely bald, and uses a cane to get around. He's also a straight-shooter, and nobody wants to be on his bad side.

He barely glances up at me as I close the office door behind me. "Computers," he grumbles. "At my age, this is like learning a new language. What's new, Will? Have you got any information on that thing we discussed?" Of course he's talking about the mayor and Morse's murder.

"Not yet," I tell him. "That's actually not why I'm here."

"I see." He swivels toward me in his chair, giving me his full attention. "Then what can I do for you?"

"Mr. Casey, you've been around forever—you know what, that came out wrong. What I mean is, you've been in Seaview Rock for a long while. I want to ask you about a business that used to be here in town about twenty years ago. It was called Buddy's Bakery."

"Ah, Buddy's." Mr. Casey smiles a little at the memory. "I haven't thought about that place in years. Best scones on the whole planet—"

"So I've heard. I also heard that the owner wasn't particularly well liked around here."

"Well, that would depend on who you asked," he says. "Good ol' Buddy. I never had a problem with him. Some other folks…" He shrugs.

"Did you know him well?"

"I knew him well enough; we weren't exactly chums or anything, but I'd pop in there almost every morning for a scone or a donut and a bit of conversation. Buddy Valencia was his name. Well, Buddy wasn't his real name; I believe it was Robert, but he'd picked up the nickname before he ever moved here."

Robert Valencia. At least the mysterious Buddy has a name now. "And the bakery was only in town for what, a couple of years?"

"That's right, two or three years he was here. And then…"

"And then one day the bakery just closed, right? Buddy left town?"

"That's the story," Mr. Casey murmurs.

"And what do you think?"

"Like I said, I haven't thought about it in years. See, Buddy was a whiz with an oven. Everything that came out of those steel doors was just magical. He was only here about a year before he was able to expand—that's why the liquor store next door to you is a double storefront."

"Buddy's baked goods were phenomenal. Tourists started coming into town just for him. Eventually, a couple of investors came to him and convinced him it would be a good idea to franchise his bakery, bring Buddy's nationwide. Seaview Rock would have been the birthplace."

"And that's why he wasn't liked? Some people in town didn't like that he was going to become what they hated?"

Mr. Casey chuckles softly. "You know, at the time I chalked it up as jealousy, the way folks treated him around here. But with everything else going on and what we've seen happen, I'm guessing you're pretty much right."

"And then one day Buddy just packed up and left, right? Abandoned the bakery and his home?"

"That's the story, yeah," Mr. Casey says again. "No one went looking for him, and most people were glad to see him go. We all took it exactly how it looked—even me. We figured he'd had enough of being an outcast."

I shake my head. "It doesn't add up, though. Sammy told me that he broke his lease and left it all behind. Someone must have looked for him—a bank, or creditors. Someone must know where he went."

"You're probably right. Someone must know."

"Mr. Casey… do you think it's possible that Buddy never left?"

He sighs slowly, understanding exactly what I mean. "Yes," he says, "I do think that's possible. But like you said, someone, somewhere, must know."

"Did he have any family around here?"

He shakes his head. "Not that I recall. Buddy was kind of a loner; I know he didn't have kids, and I don't think he was married."

"He must have had family elsewhere, then. Where did he move here from?"

"I couldn't say exactly, but he had an accent. Long Island, if I'm not mistaken." The cell phone on Casey's desk rings. "One second, Will." He answers it. "Hello? Yes. Uh-huh…" His gaze meets mine as he speaks to the caller. He says, "Well, if that's what you think is best. Alright, see you then."

He hangs up and clears his throat. "That was your girlfriend."

"Sarah?"

"Do you have more than one?" He chuckles again, but it dies quickly. "She's calling an emergency council meeting."

"Yeah, I know," I reply glumly. "For tomorrow night."

"No, Will. Tonight."

"What?!"

He nods gravely. "We both know what she's going to try to do. Now, if you say so, I'll vote against her. But I can't say the same for Holly."

"Thanks, Mr. Casey. I appreciate it. I have to go; maybe I can talk her out of this before tonight."

He shrugs. "Good luck. She's headstrong, that one."

"You can say that again."

"See you this evening, Will."

CHAPTER 11

I get into my car and immediately make the first of several calls, this one to the Runside. Holly answers on the fourth ring. I can hear the clatter of dishes and the chatter of patrons in the background.

"Holly, it's Will. Sarah is calling a council meeting for tonight to put out a proposal so that she can—"

"I know, Will," she cuts me off. "She's already called me."

"Please, Holly, please don't let it pass."

"She told me you would say that."

"Yeah, I'm saying that because it's dangerous. Not just for her, but for you and Mr. Casey as well."

"I don't know, Will. She made some good points…"

"Holly, please," I plead. "I can figure all this out. I just need some more time."

She hesitates, but eventually says, "Okay, Will."

"Great. Thank you."

As I pull out of the parking lot of Sockets & Sprockets, I try to call Sarah, but again it goes to voicemail. "Sarah, please call me back. Just tell me where you are, and we can talk. I've found out some things and I know I'm on the right track… just call me back."

I end the call and immediately ring Dennis. "Hey, Will. What's up?"

"Have you seen Sarah? Has she come back to the pet shop at all?"

"Nope, not yet."

"What about that, uh, GPS tracking thing? Can you find out where she is?"

"Sorry, Will. You can only do that if the other person authorizes it. Why, is she in trouble?"

"No." *Not yet, anyway.* "She's not taking my calls."

"Did you two have a fight or something?"

"Sort of. Listen, Dennis, I need another favor from you. I need you to look up anyone in the Long Island area with the last name Valencia, like the orange. I'm specifically looking for a Robert Valencia, but I want you to call up every person you can find and ask if they have a relative, a brother, a cousin, a son, an uncle, whatever, named Robert, goes by Buddy."

"Uh… okay. That could take a while."

"I know. I'll owe you big for this."

"Sure, Will. I'll get started now."

"Thanks, Dennis."

I hang up with him and head towards my rented house on Saltwater Drive. I figure there's only a slim chance that Sarah simply went home, but I'm not sure where else to look for her.

The next of my slew of calls is to Sammy. "Listen, I need you to do something for me," I tell him. "Go to the police station and tell Patty Mayhew you need access to the records in town hall. See if you can find anything at all on a man named Robert Valencia."

"Okay," he says. "Why?"

"That's Buddy's real name. He lived here for a few years; there must be some record of him. Plus you told me that he broke his lease, right? Someone must have looked for him after he left." *If he left at all.* "See what you can find and let me know."

"Alright, Will."

"Thanks, pal."

I pull up to the house and burst inside, hoping to find Sarah sitting on the sofa or have Rowdy bound over to me with his tail wagging, but the place is silent and empty. Then my cell phone rings.

"Will, what the heck is going on?" Karen asks loudly. "I just heard that there's an emergency town council meeting tonight. Is Sarah doing what I think she's doing?"

"Yup."

"You gotta talk her out of that."

"No kidding. I have to find her first."

"Well, I talked to her a little earlier, before I heard about all this. She said she was going home."

"I'm home now, and I can assure you that she's not… oh." She never specified which home she was going to. "I'll find her, Karen. Be at the meeting tonight?"

"I will."

I leave there and drive a bit faster than I should over to Sandbar Avenue, the street on which our new house, the one we'll be moving into in just a couple of short weeks, sits. It's a two-story colonial with dark shutters, a wide front lawn, and Sarah's car in the driveway.

I park at the curb and go around to the back, reaching over the fence to unlatch the gate. As I enter, Rowdy lets off a warning bark and then, seeing that it's me, dashes over and jumps on me, his tail swishing vigorously.

"Hey, buddy." I pet his head and then join Sarah on the deck overlooking the backyard. She sits on the wooden steps, staring out toward the back fence.

"Hey."

"Hey," she says softly.

"Can I sit here?" I ask, motioning toward the empty spot next to her.

"Sure." As I sit, she adds, "I don't have a key yet, so we've just been sitting here in the yard."

"He sure does seem to like it." I smile as Rowdy jams his snout into a patch of wildflowers.

"There's nothing you can say to talk me out of it," she tells me.

I shrug. "Can I at least try?"

"Go ahead."

"It's not just you that might get hurt. It could be Mr. Casey, or Holly."

"I know. They know, too."

"Whatever you're going to propose, I asked them not to let it pass."

"I knew you would," she says simply. "And that's okay. I think the proposition itself will stir them into action."

"And what if they call your bluff?" I ask her. "What if they realize what you're up to and decide not to do anything about it?"

She looks over at me for the first time since I've arrived and smiles, just a little. "Then I guess you'll have nothing to worry about, right?"

"I guess not."

We sit there in silence for a little while before she asks, "How are things going with the bakery mystery?"

"Oh, boy. That's..." I let out a long sigh. "That's quite a story. How about you come back to the Pet Shop Stop with me and I'll tell you all about it?"

"Maybe we can just sit here a little while longer?"

"Sure." I put my arm around her and she leans into me, and we just sit there, enjoying the spring breeze on the air in the yard of the house that'll soon be ours... assuming we're both still around in two weeks.

CHAPTER 12

Back at the pet shop, I make some more calls and ask everyone to convene here when they're done with their respective tasks. As we wait, I tell Sarah everything I learned so far about Buddy's Bakery, including Patty's suspicions that this sort of thing has been secretly happening in Seaview Rock for years, if not decades.

When I'm done, her eyes are wide and she blinks several times as she says, "You weren't kidding. That's quite a story."

"Yeah, well, we're going to find out how it ends real soon."

Karen, having not been delegated a duty, arrives first. She enters and, by way of greeting, lets off a tirade directed at Sarah. "What are you thinking? These people are lunatics, and you're just going to lure them in and hope they do something so you can try to catch them in the act? That has got to be the dumbest—"

"*Karen*," I say sharply. "That's not necessary."

"Not necessary? You two might be just as nuts as they are."

"Hey, that's hurtful," I tell her. She backs off a bit as Mr. Casey and Holly come into the pet shop.

Next, Dennis emerges from our small back storage room. "Well, it only took about twenty-five calls, but I found Buddy Valencia's sister. You're not going to believe what she had to say."

"Save it for now," I tell him. "Let's wait for Sam."

A few minutes later, Sammy joins us from his trip to town hall. He shakes his head in dismay. "I don't believe it," he tells me. "I'm no saint, but this…"

I flip the sign on the door to "closed" and lock the seven of us inside. "Alright. Some of you may be a bit fuzzy on the details, so I'm going to recap real quick. I have reason to believe that what happened to Logan Morse was not the first occurrence in Seaview Rock history—or even the second. About eighteen years ago, there was a man named Buddy who owned a bakery right next door."

"Who made really good scones," Sammy adds.

"…Right. So good, in fact, that some investors offered to help him create a franchise. The residents here didn't like it, and they made Buddy an outcast. So one day, Buddy packed up the essentials and left town. Or so it would seem. Dennis? You're up."

"Um, okay. It turns out that Buddy Valencia has a sister in Long Island. She's in her sixties, and she was pretty shocked to hear his name over the phone; it's been a long time since she's heard anything about him. The chief of police here at the time told her that Buddy had gone missing. He also told her that he'd filed a report, and that there was a full-scale manhunt underway to look for him."

"Sammy?" I ask.

He shakes his head. "There was no report. Patty searched the police database pretty thoroughly."

"Mr. Casey?" I ask. "Do you recall any search efforts for Buddy?"

"I assure you," the old man replies, "there was no such manhunt. The papers didn't report it; nobody even really talked about it."

"That's not all," Dennis says. "A few weeks after he went missing, the sister came here and collected the rest of his belongings. She met with the mayor at the time, and he convinced her that Buddy was in deep debt and had skipped town to avoid paying his bills. She said that everyone was very nice to her and spoke highly of Buddy. She had him declared legally dead after seven years; that's the minimum for the state. Never heard anything about him again, until today."

"Sammy? What else did you find?" I ask him.

He waves a sheaf of papers in his hand. "This is a copy of the minutes of a town council meeting that convened only a few days after Buddy disappeared. In it, there's an approval for a budget item to pay off the rest of the lease at 63 Center Street—where the bakery was. But it doesn't mention Buddy's name anywhere."

"So the council at the time paid off the rest of his lease using town funds?" Sarah chimes in. "And they did that before they would even know for sure if he was coming back?"

"Exactly," I say. "They knew he wasn't. Sammy, what else did you find?"

"Nothing," he tells us. "And I mean nothing. There's no mention anywhere in Seaview Rock's records of a Robert Valencia ever living here or of a business called Buddy's Bakery."

"And who was on the council at the time?" I ask.

Sammy reads from the minutes in his hand. "There were five. It was a Tammy Weis, Julian Thomas, Glenn Richter..." He looks up at me. "John Blumberg."

"So," I say loudly, starting to pace, "Buddy threatened to bring something to town that people didn't like. I think it's pretty obvious that he was killed, that someone made it look like he left town overnight, and any record of him was stricken."

"Wait," Holly interjects, rubbing her temples. "The former council, the former mayor, the former police chief... Are you telling me there was some kind of Seaview Rock 'old guard'?"

I nod. "I think that once upon a time, there were a lot more like-minded people in town than there are now, working to keep things on their idea of an even keel. I think that over time, they either died or grew senile or whatever, but there are still a few—namely, the Blumbergs. If I recall, they closed their store, what, almost ten years ago now?"

"Yes, but John Blumberg was still on the town council until about six years ago," Mr. Casey tells me.

"Which is right around the time that David Sturgess was running for mayor, before his first term," Sarah says.

"Do you think they have some kind of influence over him?" Karen asks.

"I don't know," I reply. "Of course, now we run into the same problem we had before. We can't prove any of this."

"Without records," Sammy says, "there's nothing admissible in court. I mean, there's not even a way to definitively prove that Buddy was ever really here."

"That's true," I admit. "But as Patty once told me, you don't have a case without evidence... or a confession."

"I can help with that." Karen cracks her knuckles, trying to appear menacing.

"We're not hurting anyone," I insist. "I can't believe how many times I have to tell you that."

"I guess we'll just do what you want to do," she mutters.

"Look, let me worry about that part." I glance at my watch. "It's just about time to head down to the meeting. Sarah is going to make a proposition tonight that may prompt them into some sort of action. What that might look like, I don't know, so for the foreseeable future, we're using the buddy system; no one should go anywhere alone. Don't accept anything—food, gifts—from anyone, friend or not. And I guess we'll see what happens."

"I'll ride with you," Holly says to Mr. Casey.

"Be my buddy?" Sammy asks Karen sheepishly. I can't help but wince a little.

"What about me?" Dennis asks. "There's an odd number. I have no buddy."

I let out a whistle and Rowdy comes running over, his tail moving in a helicopter spin. "Rowdy can be a buddy. Everyone ready? Let's go to a town council meeting."

SUSIE GAYLE

CHAPTER 13

O n the short drive to town hall, with Dennis and Rowdy in the backseat behind us, Sarah tells me, "You understand I'm going to say some crazy things tonight, right?"

"I'm sure you will."

"I, uh… I changed my original idea," she admits.

"Oh, so you're not going to hit them with a contemporary art gallery?"

"Not quite."

"Then what?" I ask.

"You'll see."

The council chamber isn't as packed as I've seen it on past occasions, but I'm still pretty surprised by how many people turned out for a last-minute meeting like this one. Of course, all the usual suspects are there: Mayor Sturgess sits in the very front row, looking smug and self-satisfied; a few rows behind him, Sylvia Garner sits beside Joe Miller, each of them looking a bit nervous; near the entrance at the end of a row of metal chairs is old John Blumberg, his wife Mrs. Blumberg noticeably absent.

Patty Mayhew stands just inside the double-doors leading in. She nods to me and Sarah as we enter.

A woman nearby us looks at me and scoffs. "You can't bring a dog in here!" she exclaims.

I glance down at Rowdy, who wags his tail a little. "Why not?"

"Well... because!"

I look over my shoulder at Patty and ask, "Can I bring a dog in here?"

Patty looks around and shrugs. "I don't see any signs saying you can't."

I smirk at the woman and take a seat in the back row, Dennis on one side of me and Rowdy sitting on the floor at my feet. Karen and Sammy sit in front of us, and then Mr. Casey and Holly enter, taking their place at the elevated dais facing the congregation.

After a few minutes, Sarah calls the meeting to order and initiates the Pledge of Allegiance, followed by a moment of silence for Logan Morse. After about ten seconds or so, she clears her throat.

"Many of you, if not all of you, are aware that Mr. Morse had planned to sell his land to Sprawl-Mart," she says. "And I know there's a lot of speculation around town that it was the reason for his demise. Now, I can't say anything about that for certain, but I can say that Mr. Morse was able to make that deal because of the new zoning regulations—which were part of a proposal that I wrote, and that this council passed."

She pauses and scans the room, narrowing her eyes slightly as her gaze hovers over Mayor Sturgess. "Since that tragedy, my email inbox has been flooded with inquiries about whether or not we are going to overturn that ruling. The reason I called this council meeting tonight is to tell you all, publicly... that we are *not*."

A few people murmur. I lean forward in my seat, both anxious and terrified to hear what she's going to say next.

"In fact," she says loudly over the hushed whispers of the congregation, "I believe that that type of progressive action might be precisely what this town needs." She glances over at Holly and Mr. Casey beside her, both of whom appear thoroughly confused. "As a lot of you know, I am co-owner of the Pet Shop Stop, along with Mr. Will Sullivan. Together, we have agreed to sell our location. As of tomorrow, we will be the newest store of the Pet Emporium franchise."

Oh, no.

"Thank you for your time," she says quickly as whispers rise to chatter. "We'll now open the floor to questions."

About ten people either stand up or raise their hands. A few shout randomly. Me, I'm just sitting there in disbelief.

"Is that true?" Dennis whispers to me.

"No, of course not."

"Then... why would she say that?"

"She's trying to stir the pot," I whisper back. Correction: she *has* stirred the pot, quite effectively, it would seem.

From somewhere in the chamber, a man shouts, "Can you do that?"

Sarah shrugs. "Sure. We own the building and we own the store," she says, blasé.

Of course we're not actually selling to Pet Emporium, but I understand exactly what she's doing. She knew that I would talk Mr. Casey and Holly into voting against her, so she came up with a way to anger our opposition without needing to put anything to a vote—while at the same time making herself the sole target.

Someone else shouts, "Why would you do this?"

"Look," she says loudly, "places like Sprawl-Mart and Pet Emporium aren't evil. They started out much the same way most of us have; as a single store that did well enough to warrant another one, and then another, until they evolved into a corporate chain. Obviously that means they were successful, and we want to bring that success—and revenue—into Seaview Rock."

Oh my god, she's really digging her heels in.

John Blumberg stands up and points a crooked, gnarled finger at her. "You know, some of us have worked very hard to keep this town the way it is."

Sarah smirks—she actually smirks—and says, "Oh, I think I know just how hard you've *worked*, John."

I balk. This isn't her painting a bulls-eye on her back; this is putting an apple in her mouth and climbing onto a platter.

Mr. Casey stands up and puts his hands in the air, palms out, and announces, "Alright folks, that's all the questions we're going to take. This meeting is adjourned."

More people shout to counter the shouting of the others, so Patty makes her way to the front of the chamber. "You heard the man, people. Meeting is over."

"Come on," I tell Dennis. "We need to get your sister out of here."

SUSIE GAYLE

CHAPTER 14

The ride home is silent. We drop Dennis off at his apartment and, sensing the tension, he gets out of the car with only a murmur of "Good night." Then the three of us, me, Sarah and Rowdy, make our way home to Saltwater Drive.

I pull into the driveway and park in front of the garage door, since the inside is full of packed boxes at the moment. When I cut the engine, we both sit there in silence for a long moment before Sarah says, "You understand why I had to do it that way, right?"

"I understand why you did it," I tell her, "but I don't understand why you felt you *had* to. And then, to take it further… that's just asking for more trouble."

"I know. I wanted to make sure I only had to do this once."

"Well, if they have their way, you won't be around much longer to do it again."

She gets out of the car and heads inside without another word.

"Come on, Ro." Rowdy jumps out of the car and follows me into the house.

*   *   *

I have some trouble falling asleep, my mind racing with possibilities and all the ways I could fail to keep Sarah safe from those people. Finally I drift off, and even then my slumber is plagued by nightmarish situations that involve creepy old people and a smarmy mayor.

It's still dark out when I feel a wet, cold nose on my cheek as Rowdy nudges my face.

"No, Rowdy," I mutter, "we're not going outside."

He nudges me again, more forcefully this time.

"Come on, man, let me sleep."

Then he barks right in my ear, loud enough to be a gunshot, startling me awake. "Jeez!" I exclaim as my eyes adjust to the darkness. His panting doggie face is right over mine. "What's your deal, Rowdy?"

"What's he want?" Sarah murmurs, half-asleep.

"I don't know. He's never done this before."

Sarah opens her eyes, and then a moment later suddenly sits upright in alarm. "Will," she says, "do you smell smoke?"

I sit up too and sniff the air a few times. It's faint—but it's there. And where's there's smoke…

"Get the boys. Let's go." I leap out of bed and dash for the door. We normally sleep with the bedroom door closed, but as I try to yank it open, it doesn't budge. I try again, tugging the knob with both hands. "It's jammed!" I shout. "It won't move!"

"The window!" Sarah jumps out of bed too, searching around frantically.

I throw the window open and the cool night air rushes in—and with it, an even stronger odor of something burning. I hear the screech of tires, and far down the block I see a car speeding away. I quickly grab Dennis's binoculars, which I had stuck in a half-packed box on the floor, and peer out. I see just a glimpse of the car as it speeds around the corner, tires still screaming, and off into the night.

A red coupe.

"Will!" Sarah shouts behind me. "Where's Basket?!"

"He's here. I know he's here." I get down on my hands and knees and check under the bed, then I reach in and unceremoniously pull out our three-legged cat, Basket, who yowls in protest, none too happy to be roused from sleep by a grasping hand. "Come on, get the boys. I'll go first."

Lucky for us, our bedroom window looks out over the garage, so I climb out onto the gently sloping garage roof. From there it's about an eight-foot drop to the driveway, but I parked close enough that I can hop down onto the hood of my car—denting it significantly in the process, but that's the last thing on my mind right now.

From the garage roof, Sarah lowers Basket, and then Rowdy, and finally Spark.

"Stay," I tell them. "Please."

I turn back to help Sarah down, but she disappears back through the window for a moment.

"Sarah!" I call. "What are you doing?" Through the first-floor windows, I can see the orange glow of flames consuming our kitchen.

She appears again two seconds later with a cell phone in one hand and my car keys in the other. I help her onto the car and then to the ground.

"Here. Figured we might need these."

"Thanks." I dial 911 and report the fire as Sarah stows all three pets into the backseat of my car and backs it down to the end of the driveway, a hopefully safe distance away. I get into the passenger seat to wait for the fire department to come, watching as our rented house on Saltwater Drive burns.

"Too far," Sarah says softly, staring at the flames. "Too far."

I nod in agreement, and then twist in my seat to make sure everyone is okay back there. Rowdy barks once.

"Yeah, I know. We owe you big." Rowdy probably just saved our lives; if not for him waking us, we might have remained asleep while our bedroom filled with smoke.

*   *   *

It doesn't take long for the fire department to quell the blaze, or at least it doesn't feel like long. The house is destroyed; anything that didn't burn is either smoke-damaged or water-logged, with the exception of our bedroom. The fire chief's best guess is that it started in the kitchen, since that room was completely consumed, but he assures us there will be a full investigation—especially since the bedroom doorknob was tied tightly to the closed bathroom door across the hall with nylon cord, making it impossible to open.

Patty Mayhew shows up while the firefighters are fighting the fire, but she keeps her distance and waits until the flames are out before she approaches me and Sarah.

"I'm sorry," she tells us. "Really, I am."

"Thanks, Patty. No one was hurt, and everything else was just stuff."

"How do you want to handle this?" she asks, straight-faced.

"What do you mean?"

"I mean, obviously it's going down as arson in the report. An investigation could take days, if not weeks, to come to a conclusion. If you knew anything that you wanted to tell me, I'm all ears; if not, then as a licensed private investigator in the state of Maine, I would assume that you're fully capable of getting to the bottom of this yourself. If that's what you wanted."

I raise an eyebrow. "I thought you were always a cop first, and a friend second?"

She shrugs with one shoulder. "Every rule has its exceptions."

I nod. "We didn't see or hear anything. Rowdy woke us, and we smelled smoke. When I couldn't open the door, we climbed out the window and onto the car. That's all."

"Alright. Thanks, Will. And again, I'm sorry."

"Sure."

Once she's gone, Sarah asks, "What are we going to do now?"

"First, we're going to check into a hotel. Pet-friendly, of course. Then… we're going to form a plan."

CHAPTER 15

The next morning, we leave Basket and Spark at the motel room just outside of town. I drop Sarah off on Saltwater Drive, where Karen and Sammy are waiting to help her sift through whatever she can salvage of the fire, working around the fire marshal that's investigating in the kitchen.

Then Rowdy and I head into town—not to the Pet Shop Stop, but to town hall.

As I enter, a woman at the check-in desk looks up sharply. I recognize her immediately as the same woman from the council meeting that gave me grief about Rowdy being there.

Before she can say anything, I look around and say, "I don't see any signs."

She sneers at me as I march toward the mayor's office.

The second gatekeeper is none other than Aaron Sutherland, the mayor's assistant, whose desk is positioned just outside the office. He looks up at me and says, "I'm sorry, Mayor Sturgess is not available at the moment."

I ignore him completely and push into the office, closing the door behind Rowdy and locking it from the inside.

Sturgess glances up at me from a stack of paperwork, an amused smirk on his face. "Good morning, Will. To what do I owe you, and your dog, the pleasure?"

"You win."

"I'm sorry?"

"I said, you win. It's done. The Pet Emporium thing was a lie to draw you out, and it worked. Just not the way we'd hoped. We don't want any further trouble, so… you win."

Sturgess frowns. "I'm really not sure what you're talking about, Will."

"Yes, you are. Someone set fire to our kitchen last night and rigged our bedroom door so we couldn't get out."

"Oh my," Sturgess says emphatically, frowning deeply. "I'm terribly sorry to hear that. I hope everyone is alright."

"If they weren't, we'd be having a *very* different conversation right now."

"I don't know why you would assume I had anything to do with it."

I roll my eyes. "Come on, Sturgess. Your assistant's apparently not as slick as you; I saw him speeding away down my street right after the fire started. Now, I don't know for sure, but I'm guessing that you're vetting him, just like John Blumberg did for you. Am I right?"

Sturgess says nothing, so I continue. "When you were younger, before you were mayor, Blumberg cut you in on his whole 'puritanical Seaview Rock' perspective. And in return, he became your advocate and helped you get elected. You've since returned the favor, most specifically by way of Logan Morse's murder. And now, you're doing the same thing for your young pal Aaron, right? Does he want to be mayor when he grows up?"

Sturgess folds his hands on the desk and looks me over. "Let's suppose, even for a moment, that even one iota of this is true—and I'm not saying it is. Why are you here talking to me, instead of the police?"

"Like I said," I shrug, "you win. We don't want this town rocked by another scandal. And now that your side has shown us what they're willing to do, we don't want to take any more unnecessary risks. We don't want any more deaths. We're willing to work with you."

"Even Sarah?" he asks.

"Especially Sarah." That part is not even remotely true; the reason I'm here alone is because she was afraid that she would punch the mayor right in his smarmy mouth. "Look, I've been doing my homework. I know you killed Buddy Valencia. I know you killed Logan Morse. I know about Derik Dobson, and now I know about your assistant. If I wanted you behind bars, you would be. Take that as a sign of good faith."

Sturgess stares at me quietly for a long time. Then, very slowly, he claps his hands together three times, his face breaking into a grin as he does. "Wow. I mean, just wow. They told me you were good, but sheesh! That is impressive work, Will. And to be the bigger man and come in here and open up to me like that... wow." He shakes his head. "Just think of what we could accomplish, all of us working together. This town will be perfect, just like we've always wanted it to be."

"That's the idea." I nod. "Anyway, that's, uh, that's all I wanted to say. I'll leave you to whatever it is you do."

As I turn to leave, the mayor says, "You were wrong about just one thing."

"What's that?"

"Buddy Valencia? That wasn't me."

"No?" I ask.

He shakes his head, grinning. "But everything else... like I said, wow."

I smile. "Thanks, Mayor Sturgess."

"Let's talk soon."

"Sure." I leave his office, again ignoring Aaron on the way out. Rowdy growls at him a little. As I head down the hall, I mutter to myself, "No, really, thank you Mr. Mayor." Once we're outside the town hall building, I kneel down and unclip the little silver digital recorder from Rowdy's collar. It's just a tiny thing, almost small enough to fit in the palm of my hand, that Dennis uses when he's out and about and gets inspired for a new *Bill Mulligan* comic.

And now it has about as close to a confession as we're going to come.

I wish I'd thought of it earlier, but then again, the timing wasn't right. By appealing to the mayor's sense of ego, making him think that he'd won something, that he'd gained an ally through his instruction and action, I'd gotten what I'd came for. In a way, both our plans worked; Sarah's plan paid off by forcing the other side to do something drastic (even if it meant having our house partially burnt down), and my plan paid off by managing to get a confession out of Sturgess (even if it's not quite as clear-cut as I'd hoped).

Ten minutes later I play the clip for Patty Mayhew, who listens intently to every word of the exchange between me and him. At the end of it, she looks up at me without lifting her head.

"Is it enough?" I ask eagerly.

"It's close," she says. "Is there anything else? Even just a little more to go on?"

I nod. "I can get more."

You might think I'm acting awfully calm through this whole thing for a guy that was nearly killed and his house set ablaze only hours prior. The truth is, my blood was boiling. I was enraged. Long after the fire was put out, after we'd checked into a motel and settled in and realized that no one was getting any sleep, I paced and ranted and cursed and shouted.

Then finally I realized how placid Sarah had been the entire time, sitting on the edge of the bed and patiently listening to me whine, and I said, "How on earth can you be this calm right now?!"

And Sarah stood up and hugged me and asked, "What's the use in getting angry? You're no good to anyone like this. What is it that people like to say? Don't get mad…"

"…Get even."

"Exactly."

So that's what I'm going to do. Get even.

SUSIE GAYLE

CHAPTER 16

O n the eastern side of Seaview Rock is a beige cottage-style home with an ancient-looking truck parked in the carport. I pull up to the curb and knock on the door and wait. The woman that answers wears bifocals on a chain around her neck and a shawl over her shoulders and looks to be around eighty. She smiles as she opens the door.

Then she wrinkles her nose and frowns when she notices who it is.

"You," she practically hisses.

"I know, I know. I'm still annoyingly breathing," I tell her. "Sorry about that. Can I borrow a minute of you and your husband's time?"

"No," Mrs. Blumberg says flatly.

"No? Well, Buddy Valencia, Derik Dobson, and Logan Morse say I can."

Her face goes slack—or as slack as possible for someone as wrinkled as her. (I know, you're supposed to respect your elders.

But I also believe that respect goes both ways, and these people deserve none.)

"John is out back working in the garden," she says. "We'll give you two minutes." She opens the screen door to let me in, but puts up a hand quickly when Rowdy tries to follow me. "No! The dog stays outside. He'll frighten my cat, Duke."

Well, there goes my ace in the hole. I guess that tactic won't work twice.

"That's fine," I tell her. "Rowdy, stay."

I follow her into the house, through a floral-designed living room and into a kitchen with a backdoor that leads to their small yard. She hobbles down the three wooden steps while I stand behind her near the door.

"John?" she calls out to the old man on his hands and knees in the garden. "We have a… visitor."

John Blumberg looks up and squints at me. "What do *you* want?"

"Just to talk for a few minutes."

"About how you're trying to ruin my town?" he demands.

"And about how you tried to have me killed in turn."

He scoffs and resumes harvesting his cucumbers. "You have no proof."

"You're right, I don't. Not about that, anyway. Do you remember a fellow named Buddy Valencia?"

Mr. Blumberg looks at his wife quickly, and then back to me. "Nope. Doesn't ring a bell."

"Are you sure?" I ask. "Because from what I hear, he used to be your shop neighbor, or whatever you call it, about eighteen years ago. Apparently he made the best scones on the planet."

"They weren't *that* good," he mutters.

"Oh, so you do remember him?" I ask. "Because Buddy was doing pretty well for himself. Then Buddy disappeared. And I find it really odd that you and your council paid off his lease only three days later. It's like you knew he wasn't coming back."

"That was almost twenty years ago," he insists. "I barely remember it."

"Sure, I understand. There were so many others, right?"

John Blumberg, with some difficulty, stands. "Just what are you trying to say, Mr. Sullivan?"

"I'm saying that you and your wife are murderers, Mr. Blumberg," I tell him plainly. "I know that you two sent Sarah the cupcakes laced with cyanide. Depending on how long you've been favoring rat poison, maybe that's how you did in poor Buddy, too. Would've been pretty easy, right? Sharing a wall like that?" I eye up his cucumbers and take a calculated risk. "In fact, last time I was here, Mrs. Blumberg mentioned that she'd been doing her own pickling for about twenty years now. I can't think of a better place to hide a body than your own garden."

Mr. Blumberg almost laughs. "You can't dig up my garden! You don't have the authority."

"You're right, I don't." I pull out my cell phone. "But the police are waiting for my call. And no offense, John, but you're kind of up there in years. I don't think you can dig Buddy up before they get here."

"No," John Blumberg says, his eyes growing wide as he shakes his head. "You're suspended. The police arrested you. You're not even supposed to be here!"

I shrug. "Maybe. Let's see what Patty has to say." I press a button on my phone.

"Wait, wait, wait," John insists. "Hang on, Will." He puts on a big fake smile. "We can work something out here, I think."

I lower my phone. "Like what?"

He looks at his wife for help, his eyes pleading.

"We have influence," she says. "We can help you."

"Not anymore." I make the call.

*   *   *

Patty Mayhew has a pretty busy day. First she arrests Mayor Sturgess and his assistant, Aaron Sutherland, on counts of murder and arson, respectively. Then she has a team excavate the entire Blumberg backyard until they find the bones that most likely belong to one Robert "Buddy" Valencia, buried about five and a half feet underground.

And while digging, they find the remains of three others.

Forensic testing can take a while, but I'm pretty confident that the bodies they've discovered will match the people that went missing over the last thirty-something years, people that allegedly skipped town or plain disappeared.

Naturally, the Blumbergs are arrested. I don't know what's going to happen to them, considering their age, but I hope it's terrible.

*   *   *

I knock on Georgia Strauss's door. She opens it and simply says, "I heard. Well done, Will."

"Georgia, you owe me like, a thousand dollars."

She smirks. She actually smirks, one of the first times I've ever seen a genuine smile on her face. "Come in." I follow her in. Her home is warm and inviting, not overly decorous or lavish. "Let me find my checkbook."

"I don't want your money, Georgia."

She turns sharply with one manicured eyebrow raised. "Oh?"

"No. I just want the truth. I found your 'scones' for you. You knew about Buddy Valencia, but you couldn't just tell me. Why not? What's the connection?"

"That wasn't part of our deal."

"You're right. You pointed me in the right direction; you don't owe me any answers. But let me tell you what I know. Eighteen years ago, there were five members of town council: Tammy Weis, Julian Thomas, Glenn Richter, John Blumberg… and

Georgia Strauss." Earlier, when Sammy read from the council minutes from all those years ago, he'd left her name off on purpose, knowing that I was working with her. But I had gotten a look at the document for myself.

She doesn't say anything, but her shoulders droop a bit resignedly.

"Were you involved?" I ask.

"I didn't know what was happening."

"I don't believe that."

She turns and sighs. "Fine. I had an inkling, but… I chose to ignore it."

"So this is some sort of atonement?"

"The mistakes of history are doomed to be repeated unless someone intervenes," she tells me. "I didn't want that to happen to anyone else."

I nod slowly. Regardless of what I think of her right now, I understand her position. "I'm not going to take anything from you, Georgia. And you're not going to take anything from me anymore—not my time, not my resources. I think we're done here."

"That seems fair." She lowers her gaze to the floor and asks, "Are you going to… for lack of a better term, tell on me?"

"I thought about it, but… no. I'm not going to. You have to live with the decisions you've made."

"You're right. I do."

I start toward the door to leave when she adds, "By the way… your suspension was overturned."

"Goodbye, Georgia."

SUSIE GAYLE

CHAPTER 17

"This is nice," Sarah says with a content sigh.

"It sure beats a motel." The two of us sit on plastic folding chairs on our new deck, behind our new house at 1442 Sandbar Avenue. Basket lies under Sarah's chair, basking in the shade, while Spark and Rowdy chase each other through the yard, trampling wildflowers and marking their newfound territory.

Someday soon we'll get decent outdoor furniture, but that'll have to wait until the insurance money comes through. In the meantime, we had to replace most of our indoor furniture and a lot of belongings. The only things really salvageable from the fire were the contents of our bedroom and, fortunately, the stuff that Sarah had already packed up and stowed in the garage.

And sure, we had to spend a week in a motel with our three beasts, but Karen came through and managed to get the closing date pushed up eight days to get us in the new house faster. And yeah, my credit card statement is going to be painful to look at later this month, but the fire marshal definitively ruled it an arson, so that should expedite things a bit.

Like Sturgess said, I was right about almost everything. When presented with the evidence of arson, Aaron Sutherland broke down sobbing and admitted to setting fire to our rented house by blowing out the pilot light in the oven, turning on the gas and lighting a candle. The Blumbergs refused to admit to anything and, as far as I know, are still seeking a plea of not guilty, but they'll have a very difficult time explaining all the bones dug up in their garden.

Sturgess is still being stubborn as well, even after hearing the half-confession that I recorded in his office. First he tried to claim that it was illegal to record someone without their knowledge, but technically I'm an officer of the state, so that wouldn't fly. It was actually Kyle Morse that put the nail in his coffin; only two days ago, Morse turned himself in for being an accessory to his father's murder. Apparently he had orchestrated the meeting between Logan and Sturgess at the Runside, where Sturgess had walloped his friend over the head with a jack handle.

Patty spent a few days interrogating various community members, including Sylvia Garner and Joe Miller, to find out just how far their involvement went, but it seems that the real culprits were limited to those five. A handful of other people suspected what had happened, but said nothing. With no real culpability, Patty let them slide—albeit with a very stern warning that this was over.

I'd say "all's well that ends well," but with people dead and almost a half-dozen arrests, there's really nothing well about it, other than knowing that it's done and we can all look toward the future now.

"Oh!" Sarah says suddenly. "What time is it? We have to get to the meeting soon!"

I groan. "Do we have to? It's so nice out. Can't we fake our deaths or something?"

Sarah laughs. "Maybe next month. It's Mr. Casey's first public address; we need to be there to support him."

"Fine." I let out an exaggerated grunt of effort as I get up, just so she's aware of how little I want to go to another town council meeting.

*   *   *

Sarah takes her place on the dais beside Mr. Casey and Holly as I find a seat next to Sammy and Karen, who no doubt came together. And you know what? That's fine. They're adults. They can do as they please.

Dennis comes in, wearing his usual black beanie, and takes a seat beside me. "Hey," he whispers. "The new issue of *Bill Mulligan* will be out in a few days."

I can't help but grin. "Glad to hear it, Dennis. I can't wait to see what you've come up with."

In minutes, the assembly chamber is standing-room only, and Holly calls the meeting to order. I'm learning an awful lot about local politics lately. For example, I didn't know that according to the Seaview Rock town charter, if a mayor is incapacitated, dies, or otherwise cannot perform his duties (like if he's arrested and charged with murder) it's up to the current council to appoint an interim mayor to carry out the remainder of his term.

You would think that would be a lengthy process and a careful deliberation, but Holly and Sarah immediately knew who to choose, and they chose Barton Casey.

After the Pledge of Allegiance and the review of last month's minutes, Sarah introduces Mr. Casey—sorry, Mayor Casey—and invites him to say a few words. A silence so profound that I can hear my own heartbeat falls over the assembly hall as Casey stands.

"You know," he begins, "I'm not a politician. But I've accepted this responsibility, and I'm going to carry it out to the best of my ability for the next year and three months. I'm also going to remain on the council, in order to ensure that these two branches of our local government work together in a way that serves the town's best interests.

"I'm not a politician, but maybe that's not what we need right now. I'm not going to talk in circles; I'm not going to ingratiate myself to anyone; I'm not going to make any promises that we can't keep. Most importantly, I'm going to be honest. And I'm going to start right now.

"What's been happening in Seaview Rock over the last... decades, really, have been scandals and secrets and borderline conspiracies. All that, everything, ends now. Changes are coming to this little town, and they're going to be the changes we need. If you don't like it, then leave. These changes are about what's best for everyone, not to service a few.

"To prove our point, me and the other members of council have agreed that the first thing we're going to do with our newfound control is... well, we're going to relinquish control. Tonight we'll be introducing a proposition that will allow all Seaview Rock residents to have a voice. Anything we want to pass will be published beforehand on the town's website, and it will be put to a vote by everyone present at the next meeting." He looks around at the packed room and adds, "Obviously, that means we're going to need to expand this hall a bit."

A few people chuckle at that. Of course I already knew about all this, but still I nod approvingly along with dozens of other people around me, some murmuring their assent and smiling at the notion.

"Oh, and one more thing," Mayor Casey says. "I'm not going to use that ridiculous mayoral office. If you want to find me, I'll be at my cramped little desk at Sockets & Sprockets, pecking away at that confounded keyboard. Thank you." He turns to Holly and Sarah and says, "Thank you." Lastly, he turns and looks directly at me, smiles a little, and says, "Thank *you*."

The entire assembly hall stands and delivers a rousing round of applause as he takes his seat again. Looks like things are going to be different now, and maybe it was a bumpy road to get there, but I think Seaview Rock will be okay.

You know what? I'm just going to say it anyway. All's well that ends well.

THE END

Made in the USA
Middletown, DE
10 June 2017